# WHAT GREAT THING CAN PATCHES DO?

By Sharon K. Mitchell

Illustrated by Douglas Kimball

Summary:
Patches, a dog adopted from an animal shelter, discovers that he has the greatest thing of all to offer others as he tries to find his place in the world.

ISBN  0-9772222-0-9
Copyright 2005 by Sharon K. Mitchell
Library of Congress Control Number 2001012345


Published by Kobz
United States of America

First printing 2005


Printed in China by TSE Worldwide Press, Inc.
Ontario, California  91761

# Dedicated to Patches

*1986-1998*
*faithful friend*

Eight-year-old Katie wanted a special puppy that would be just right for her. One Saturday morning, she visited Dogtown's shelter for the homeless and saw several puppies. One puppy was smaller and shyer than all the rest. He was black all over except for a couple of little white patches of fur on his chest. When Katie picked him up and held him snuggly, she immediately loved him. "I'm going to call you Patches," Katie said, "and you're coming home with me."

Over the next three years, Katie and Patches developed the closest kind of friendship. Patches seemed to be quite happy, but on one particular day, he was not feeling good about himself. His mind was filled with thoughts of all the great things that other dogs could do. So he began to share these thoughts with Katie.

Patches began …

"Katie, you know Showdown Shepherd who works for Dogtown's K-9 force? Last summer, when Feral Fox tried to break into Happy Hen's house, he was stopped in his tracks by Showdown Shepherd at her doorway. At first, he just smiled at Feral Fox and showed him his pretty white teeth. Then he growled deeply and barked ferociously. Everybody knows that when Showdown Shepherd barks, Dogtown listens. Feral Fox certainly listened. He left nothing behind his scampering feet but a cloud of dust as he fled for his life."

Patches thought to himself, "That was a great thing that Showdown Shepherd did, but what great thing can I do?"

**showdown** - *A happening that forces something to come to an end.*
**feral** - *A wild animal.*
**ferociously** – *In a very dangerous way.*

"Katie, I remember the article that was in the *Dogtown Bark* about Boasting Beagle's remarkable talent. When Bouncing Bunny wandered off from home and got himself lost in the woods, it was Boasting Beagle who found him. He said that he can find anybody when he puts his nose to the ground. After Bouncing Bunny was returned home safely, Boasting Beagle wagged his tongue all over Dogtown about his keen senses and magnificent tracking abilities. He claimed that all his ancestors were blue-ribbon hunters. You know, Katie, I don't believe there have ever been any hunters in my family."

Patches thought to himself, "That was a great thing that Boasting Beagle did in finding Bouncing Bunny, but what great thing can I do?"

**boasting -** *Bragging about oneself to others.*

"Katie, Relentless Retriever can swim better than anybody I know.  I'll never forget the time when Blind Bat lost his glasses while flying over PeekaPoo's pond.  Blind Bat didn't know how to swim, and he didn't remember where in the pond he had dropped his glasses.  When Relentless Retriever heard that disturbing news, she dove into that pond and tore it up until she finally found those glasses tangled in some thick green algae. Blind Bat was beside himself when he got his glasses back."

Patches thought to himself, "That was a great thing that Relentless Retriever did, but what great thing can I do?"

**relentless** - *To keep on going without stopping.*
**retriever** - *One that finds something and carries it back.*

Patches continued his story…

"Bulky Bernard doesn't let anybody or anything ruffle his fur. He stays calm no matter what. I remember that January blizzard Dogtown had while Kid Kangaroo was visiting here from Paradise Plains. In his excitement of seeing snow for the first time, Kid Kangaroo played leap hop until he got himself buried heels over head in snow. When Bulky Bernard heard his cries for help, he grabbed him by his legs and rescued him from the heavy heaps. That's how he got to be Top Dog."

Patches thought to himself, "That was a great thing that Bulky Bernard did, but what great thing can I do?"

**bulky** – *Very large.*

"Katie, that Daring Dachshund is always into something. Just last Saturday, while Mishap Monkey was playing with his autographed baseball, it rolled into the middle of a drainpipe. Mishap Monkey used everything from a broken rake to water from a leaky hose to reach the baseball, but the ball would not move. As it turned out, Daring Dachshund was able to squeeze his long body through that narrow pipe and recover the baseball. Everybody is always saying that he can do anything."

Patches thought to himself, "That was a great thing that Daring Dachshund did, but what great thing can I do?"

**daring** – *Willing to do something that is risky or that requires courage.*
**mishap** – *Carelessness.*

"You know, Katie, if there is a tornado coming, Coach Collie is a good one to have around. I remember when his Little League Lambs gave him a surprise birthday party at Whirling Wind Acres. As they were all playing soccer, it started getting really dark. Everybody was scattered on the field when Coach Collie saw a black funnel cloud in the distance. A powerful tornado was headed straight for them! So Coach Collie blew his whistle and quickly rounded up his Little League Lambs. Then he herded them into a nearby ravine. That ravaging tornado passed right over their heads, but because of Coach Collie, everybody was safe."

Patches thought to himself, "That was a great thing that Coach Collie did, but what great thing can I do?"

**ravine** - *A deep narrow valley.*
**ravaging** - *To bring about destruction.*

"Katie, I'll never forget the time when Tenacious Terrier and Howling Hound were returning from a hunting trip. Tenacious Terrier spotted Armo Adillo stealing vegetables from Chef Chow's garden. Armo Adillo didn't think that anybody would ever recognize him because he always did his digging at night. That night, he got caught.

**tenacious** – *Holding something tightly without letting go.*
**chow** – *1. A dog breed which originated from China. 2. Food.*

21

Tenacious Terrier called Armo Adillo a little rat. Then he grabbed him by the tail and would not let go. In the meantime, Howling Hound bayed loudly for Showdown Shepherd to come to the scene. Before Armo Adillo could make any fast moves, Showdown Shepherd had him claw-cuffed and out of there. Since that night, Armo Adillo has really changed his ways. He now has planted his own garden because he learned that it is not right to steal."

      Patches thought to himself, "That was a great thing that Howling Hound and Tenacious Terrier did, but what great thing can I do?"

**bayed** – *A deep prolonged bark.*

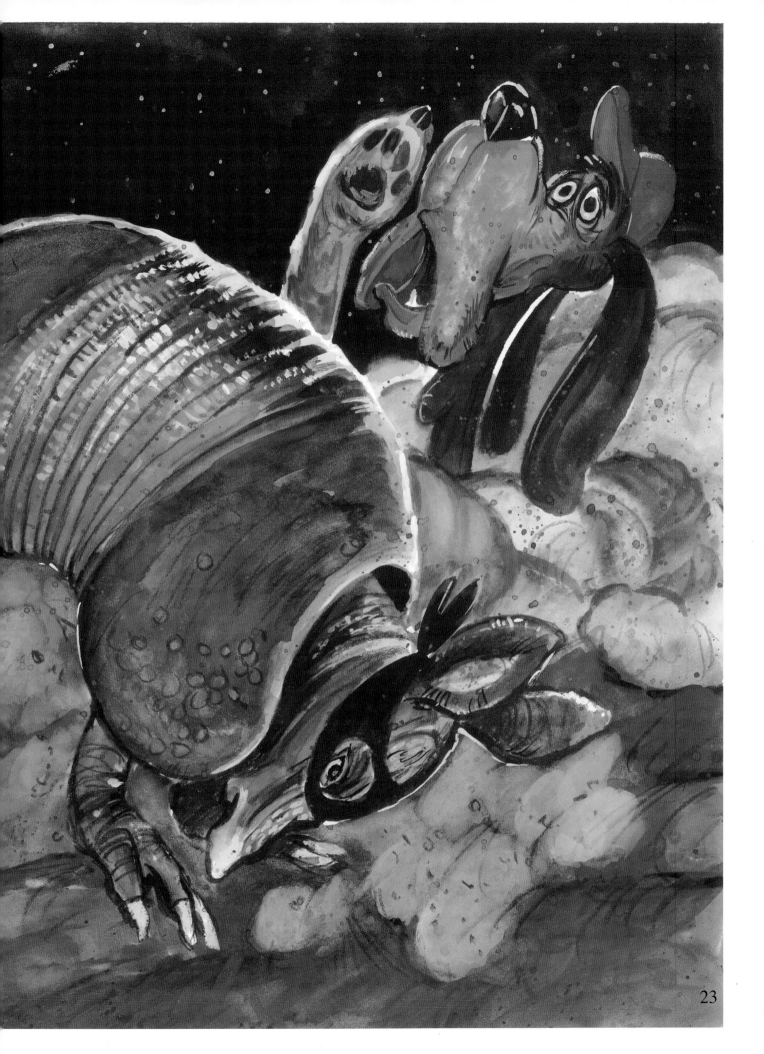

Patches then sadly declared, "Katie, I never did anything great. I don't know how to do all the great things everybody else has done."

Katie replied, "Don't think about the things that you cannot do. You don't have to do things like Showdown Shepherd, Daring Dachshund, Tenacious Terrier, or all the others to be great. Patches, you are very special, and I wouldn't change anything about you. You are great because of who you are. So just be you."

"Who am I?" asked Patches.

Katie answered, "You wait faithfully by the door for me to come home from school so that you can greet me with a hug. You are **Patient Patches.**"

**patient** – *Able to remain calm while waiting.*

25

"You are truly grateful for anything given to you, and you consider the needs of others before your own. You are **Polite Patches**."

"You quickly forgive me when I sometimes don't take you to Dogtown Park. If you don't get your way, you never hold a grudge. You are **Pardoning Patches**."

**pardoning** – *Totally forgiving somebody for something.*

"When your younger cousins visit us, you allow them to play with your stuffed toys.  You never whine or complain if some of your toys become tattered or torn.  You are **Peaceful Patches**."

"If I don't always wake up in the morning when I should, you continue to gently nudge my face until you see my sleeping eyes open. You are **Persevering Patches**."

**persevering** - *Completing a job even when feeling discouraged.*

29

"You often visit Dogtown's shelter and share your snack bones with the homeless. You are **Precious Patches**."

...and help Blind Bat
to see better,
and bless Armo Adillo's
new garden,
and Mishap Monkey –
well, he needs help
with everything,
and...

"You are filled with love, and you always show that love.  So to me,
you are **Perfect Patches**."

As Patches understood Katie's words, his heart was filled with joy.

"I discovered the great thing that I can do!" Patches exclaimed. "I can love you and others, Katie!"

So from that day on, Patches never again compared himself to other dogs, for he had learned that his life is filled with love, and that love is the greatest thing of all.

# About the Author

**Sharon K. Mitchell** *has written this book with the purpose of inspiring children to discover that the meaning of character is not based solely upon one's abilities or talents, but rather, notable character is developed by one's love from the heart. Currently residing in Maryville, Tennessee, she was an educator in South Mississippi public schools for 25 years. Her bachelor of science degree was received from the University of Southern Mississippi and her master of education degree from William Carey College. As a lover of animals, she used her beloved pet of many years, Patches, as the central focus of this tender story.*

# About the Illustrator

**Douglas Kimball**, *who has always loved to draw and paint since his childhood, has been a professional artist for 25 years. He received his bachelor of fine arts degree from Ball University in Muncie, Indiana, and his master of fine arts degree from Syracuse University in New York. In addition to illustrating books, he has a variety of art interests ranging from painting portraits to landscapes. He currently resides in Knoxville, Tennessee, with his wife, three children, and a Weimaraner named Jed.*